HECTOR SYLVESTER

Alan Durant
& Ant Parker

Collins
A Division of HarperCollinsPublis

D1494458

Hector Sylvester marched through the jungle. He was **bold** and he was **brave.** Out slithered...

But Hector Sylvester did not cower.
Hector Sylvester did not quake.
He opened his mouth and went,

Then the slippery, slimy snake
slid away.

Hector Sylvester stamped through the jungle. He was **mighty** and he was **mean**. Out crawled...

...a **CROCODILE**, a snippy, snappy crocodile.

But Hector Sylvester did not cower. Hector Sylvester did not quake. He opened his mouth and went,

Then the snippy, snappy crocodile crept away.

Hector Sylvester strode through the jungle. He was **tough** and he was **tall**. Out sprang...

...a **LION**, a big, bad lion.

But Hector Sylvester did not cower.
Hector Sylvester did not quake.
He opened his mouth and went,

Then the big, bad lion ran away.

Hector Sylvester swaggered through the jungle. He was **Chief** and he was **King**.

But, then, down dangled...

...a spider, an incey-wincey spider! Hector Sylvester stopped quite still.

Hector Sylvester quaked and he cowered.

The spider came closer.
Hector Sylvester quailed and
he quivered. Hector Sylvester
went very pale.

The spider came closer. He came right up to Hector Sylvester and...

...tickled him under the nose!

"He, he, *he*," went Hector Sylvester.
"Ho, *ho*, ho," went Hector Sylvester.

Then out came the big, bad lion, and the slippery, slimy snake and the snippy, snappy crocodile.

Did they **roar?**
Did they **hiss?**
Did they **snap?**

NO!

with the incey-wincey spider
and Hector Sylvester.

They giggled and they tickled,
they tickled and they giggled,

For Max Lyon (roar!)
AD
For Luke and Lotty
AP

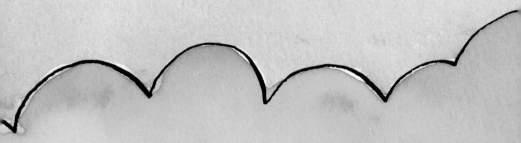

Also available by
Ant Parker and Alan Durant:
SNAKE SUPPER

First published in Great Britain by HarperCollins Publishers Ltd in 1996. 10 9 8 7 6 5 4 3 2 1
First published in Picture Lions in 1996. 10 9 8 7 6 5 4 3 2 1
Picture Lions is an imprint of the Children's Division, part of HarperCollins Publishers Limited,
77-85 Fulham Palace Road, Hammersmith, London W6 8JB. Text copyright © Alan Durant 1996.
Illustrations copyright © Ant Parker 1996. The author and illustrator assert the moral right to
be identified as the author and illustrator of the work. A CIP catalogue record for this book is
available from the British Library. ISBN 0 00 198187 0 (HB) ISBN 0 00 664586 0 (PB) All rights reserved.
No part of this publication may be reproduced, stored in a retrieval system, or transmitted in any form
or by any means, electronic, mechanical, photocopying, recording or otherwise, without the prior
permission of HarperCollins Publishers Ltd. Printed in Hong Kong